Usborne
Stargazing Book

Sam Smith

Illustrated by Lee Cosgrove

Designed by Karen Tomlins

Astronomy Consultant: Ed Bloomer,
Royal Observatory Greenwich

The Northern and Southern Hemispheres have their seasons at opposite times of year and also have different views of the stars. **This is a guide to stargazing in the Northern Hemisphere,** but you can still use many of the same tips and tricks to stargaze anywhere.

USBORNE QUICKLINKS

For links to websites where you can watch stargazing videos and find helpful tips and activities, scan the QR code or go to usborne.com/Quicklinks and type in this book's title.

Usborne Publishing is not responsible for the content or availability of external websites. Children should be supervised online. Please follow the online safety guidelines at usborne.com/Quicklinks

Star patterns are shown using yellow, five-pointed stars, but in the night sky the stars will look like twinkling dots of light. Any stars shown in backgrounds are only for decoration.

STARRY NIGHTS

On clear, dark nights, the sky is lit up by thousands of beautiful stars — giant balls of very hot gas so, SO far away that they look like tiny, twinkling dots.

For millions of years, people have seen patterns in the stars, imagining lines that join them up. These "dot-to-dot" pictures are called CONSTELLATIONS.

For a long time, astronomers have used constellations to map the night sky...

Canis Minor

Hydra

...and sailors have used them to find their way at sea.

Canis Major

Throughout history, many cultures have created their own unique constellations, seeing different patterns in the same stars.

The Ancient Greeks created their constellations from their myths — epic tales of gods, heroes and monsters. Those constellations have proved so popular that many people still use them today.

Orion

Taurus

You can find out more about these constellations on pages 20–21.

So, are you ready to learn the ancient art of reading the stars?

WHERE AND WHEN?

You'll need dark, clear skies for a good evening of stargazing. Try to plan what you want to see before you leave, and always go with a grown-up.

Look at the weather forecast to check it won't be cloudy. If it is, you might not see any stars.

Because the Moon is so bright, the best times to stargaze are when it's just a thin crescent, or when you can't see the Moon at all.

City lights also make stars harder to see, and buildings and trees can block your view...

...so try to go to an open or high-up space away from as many lights as you can.

Most stars only appear in certain seasons, but one pattern leaps out in the northern sky all year: the Big Dipper.

You may hear some people call the Big Dipper "the Plough".

DID YOU KNOW?
The Big Dipper can help you find fainter patterns, or constellations whose shapes are a bit tricky to imagine. Find out how on pages 12–13.

WHAT TO TAKE:

A backpack

Snacks and a hot drink

A phone and a compass

A flashlight

Warm clothes

Binoculars

A grown-up

WHAT WILL YOU SEE?

Objects in space are all incredibly far away. So what do they look like to us at such great distances from planet Earth?

The Moon is closest to us, so it looks biggest and brightest. It changes from a thin crescent to a full circle, and back again, each month.

Saturn

Other planets are millions of miles further away than the Moon, so they look much smaller, like bright dots.

When you look up at the sky, the planet Saturn will look like a small yellow dot. It can only be seen in detail with extremely powerful telescopes.

The stars are so far away that it takes years for their light to reach your eyes. They're the smallest dots of all in the night sky.

The stars in constellations only appear to be near each other from Earth. But some stars do exist in groups, forming beautiful clusters. The cluster in this photo is called the Pleiades.

BLUE, WHITE AND RED

If you look closely, you'll see that some stars are different colors. That's because there are **many types of stars**. The hottest ones look blue or white, but cooler ones look red.

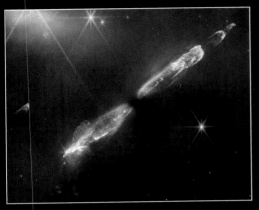

The James Webb Space Telescope took this photo of a newly born star in 2023.

WHITE DWARF
The dying, Earth-sized remains of a star like our Sun.

RED DWARF
The most common star type, but none is big and bright enough to see from Earth with the naked eye.

YELLOW DWARF
A star like our Sun. Most look white, not yellow.

RED GIANT
An old star that has gotten much bigger. Our Sun will become one in five billion years, possibly engulfing the Earth!

BLUE SUPERGIANT
A large, very hot star. Some of them are millions of times brighter than our Sun.

RED HYPERGIANT
The biggest known star type. Some are so big that *billions* of stars the size of our Sun could fit inside them!

BLUE HYPERGIANT
Huge and bright, these stars don't live long compared to others (only millions of years, not billions).

DID YOU KNOW?
Your eyes can make out about 4,000 stars on a dark night.

There are many other types of stars too. The ones shown here are not to scale as the differences between smaller stars and bigger ones are so enormous that we'd run out of space on the page!

THE CHANGING NIGHT SKY

The Earth is constantly spinning — that's why the Sun rises and sets in our sky, giving us day and night. But at night you can see the stars slowly move across the sky too.

Stars appear in one place as night begins to fall...

The constellation Gemini
early in the evening

...but by dawn, they will have crept around to a different part of the sky.

Gemini later the same night

TRY THIS...

Pick out a star above a tree or building. If you look for it again a few hours later, it will have moved somewhere else. It may even have dipped below the horizon and vanished completely.

A GUIDING LIGHT

There's one star that never moves. Its name is Polaris, but most people call it the North Star because it shows the way north.

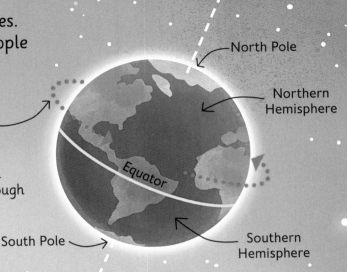

North Star

North Pole

Northern Hemisphere

Direction of Earth's spin

Equator

South Pole

Southern Hemisphere

The Earth spins around an imaginary line that passes through its North and South poles.

DID YOU KNOW?
There isn't a "South Star" at the opposite end of the line — it's just good luck that the North Star is in the right place to be so useful!

Because the North Star is on the imaginary line through the Earth, it stays still like the middle of a starry merry-go-round.

The North Star is only visible from the Northern Hemisphere — the Earth's top half. You can find it from the Big Dipper like this:

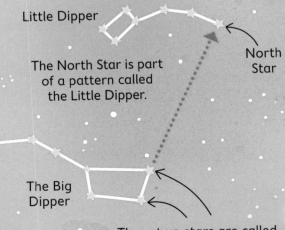

Little Dipper

The North Star is part of a pattern called the Little Dipper.

North Star

The Big Dipper

These two stars are called "the Pointers" as they always point to the North Star.

This photo, taken over several hours, shows how the stars in the Northern Hemisphere turn counterclockwise around the North Star.

9

SEASONAL SKIES

The Sun is our home star. Each year the Earth travels all the way around it in a path called an *orbit*. As it does, the seasons change, and so do the stars you can see.

The arrows in this picture show how the Earth's night-time side faces in different directions throughout the year. That's why you can see different stars.

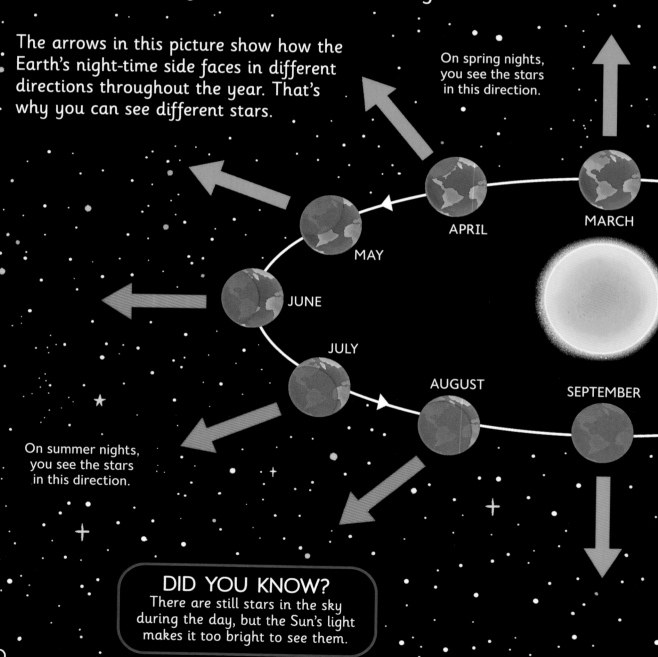

On spring nights, you see the stars in this direction.

MARCH

APRIL

MAY

JUNE

JULY

AUGUST

SEPTEMBER

On summer nights, you see the stars in this direction.

DID YOU KNOW?
There are still stars in the sky during the day, but the Sun's light makes it too bright to see them.

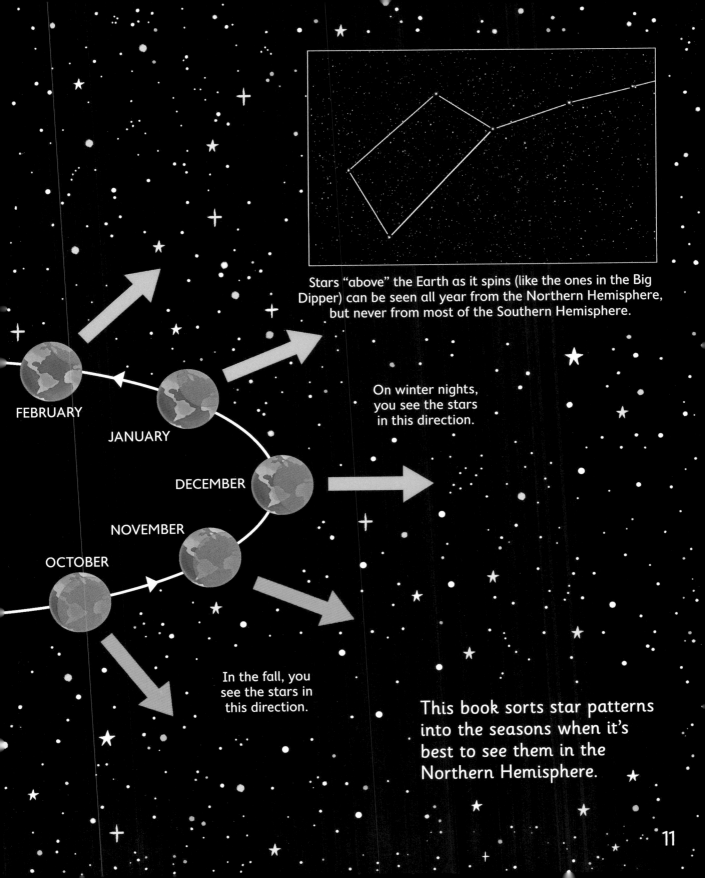

Stars "above" the Earth as it spins (like the ones in the Big Dipper) can be seen all year from the Northern Hemisphere, but never from most of the Southern Hemisphere.

FEBRUARY

JANUARY

DECEMBER

NOVEMBER

OCTOBER

On winter nights, you see the stars in this direction.

In the fall, you see the stars in this direction.

This book sorts star patterns into the seasons when it's best to see them in the Northern Hemisphere.

11

USING THE BIG DIPPER

Because you can easily see the Big Dipper in the north all year round, it makes a very useful signpost for finding star patterns in any season.

You can think of the brightest stars as stepping stones. Starting from the Big Dipper, jump between them with your eyes. This is called STAR HOPPING.

CYGNUS

7 fists

BOÖTES

3 fists

THE BIG DIPPER

3 fists

5 fists

LEO

DID YOU KNOW?
You can use your fists to help judge distances as you star hop. Find out how with the handy trick on the right.

TRY THIS...
Find the Big Dipper (in Ursa Major) on the star maps on pages 28–31. Then use the arrows on this page to see how you can begin star hopping from it to each season's constellations.

A HANDY TRICK

The night sky above us is like a giant semicircle, and a semicircle can be split up into 180 *degrees* (°). You can use your hands to measure how many degrees apart stars are to help you "hop" more accurately.

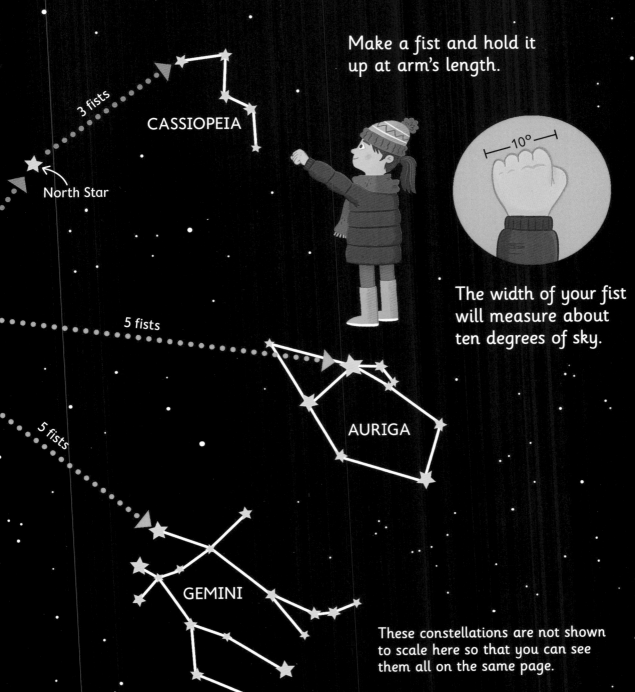

Make a fist and hold it up at arm's length.

├— 10° —┤

3 fists

CASSIOPEIA

North Star

5 fists

5 fists

AURIGA

GEMINI

The width of your fist will measure about ten degrees of sky.

These constellations are not shown to scale here so that you can see them all on the same page.

SPRING STARS

In the spring night sky, you can see all of these constellations, which are based on Ancient Greek myths.

LEO

The hero Heracles (Hercules) defeated this giant lion in a long battle. The king of the gods, Zeus, was so impressed that he placed the lion among the stars.

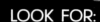
Regulus

LOOK FOR:
the head section, shaped like a backwards question mark, with its brightest star, Regulus, at the bottom.

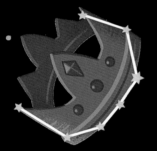

CORONA BOREALIS

Princess Ariadne wore this crown when she married the god Dionysus. Her new husband was so happy that he hurled it up high into the sky.

LOOK FOR:
the semicircle of stars next to Boötes.

LOOK FOR:
the Big Dipper, which makes up the Great Bear's tail.

URSA MAJOR

One day, Zeus's wife, Hera, heard that he'd had a son with a woman named Callisto. The goddess was so furious that she turned Callisto into this great bear.

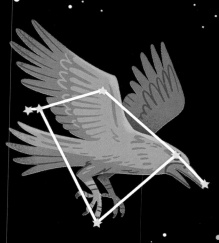

CORVUS

This crow was once white, but one day it delivered some bad news to Apollo. In his rage, the sun god put a curse on the bird, darkening its feathers forever.

LOOK FOR:

the kite shape near the bright star Spica, in Virgo.

VIRGO

Virgo is the goddess of justice. She grew tired of human unfairness on Earth and so flew away up into the heavens.

LOOK FOR:

its brightest star, Spica, which is 3 fists away from Arcturus in Boötes.

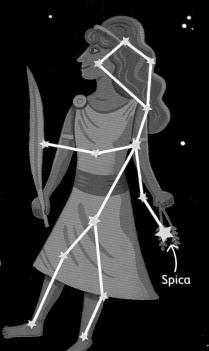

Spica

LOOK FOR:

the ice-cream-cone shape near the Big Dipper, with the bright red star Arcturus at its base.

Boötes is pronounced "bo-OH-tees".

Arcturus

BOÖTES

Legends say that Boötes was a shepherd whom the gods placed in the stars to reward him for inventing the first plow.

To see the positions of these constellations, turn to the star maps on page 28.

SUMMER STARS

The bright constellations in the summer night sky are ideal to practice star hopping.

CYGNUS
When Zeus fell in love with Queen Leda of Sparta, he turned himself into this swan so that he could meet her in secret.

Deneb

LOOK FOR:
the cross shape with Deneb, its brightest star, at one end.

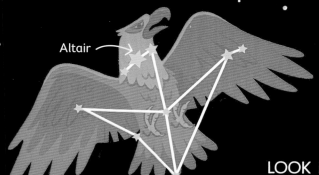

Altair

AQUILA
This great eagle belonged to Zeus, and swooped from the heavens to carry his thunderbolts to Earth.

LOOK FOR:
its brightest star, Altair, about 4 fists away from Deneb, in Cygnus.

SAGITTARIUS
Sagittarius is a centaur (a creature that's half human and half horse). The arrow in his bow is aimed at Antares, "the heart of Scorpius."

LOOK FOR:
the teapot-like shape, which makes up the centaur's bow and arrow.

LYRA

Orpheus was a musician who could charm all living things, and even rocks, with his beautiful music. Lyra was his harp.

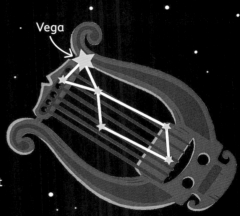

Vega

LOOK FOR:
the little slanted rectangle, and Lyra's brightest star, Vega, about 3 fists from Deneb, in Cygnus.

HERCULES

The hero Hercules (Heracles to the Greeks) performed 12 impossibly difficult tasks, including slaying the Hydra – a monstrous sea serpent.

LOOK FOR:
the four-cornered shape in the middle, which is a star pattern called the **Keystone**.

SCORPIUS

This scorpion stung and killed a mighty hunter named Orion. You can see Orion himself in the winter stars on page 21.

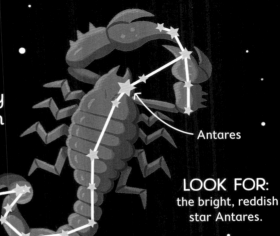

Antares

LOOK FOR:
the bright, reddish star Antares.

To see the positions of these constellations, turn to the star maps on page 29.

FALL STARS

In the fall, the nights begin to get longer, and the sky quickly fills up with lots of bright stars to look for.

CASSIOPEIA

This vain queen boasted that she was prettier than the daughters of Poseidon, the sea god. Poseidon was furious, and sent a terrible sea monster named Cetus to destroy her city.

LOOK FOR:
the big "W" (or "M") shape, always on the opposite side of the North Star to the Big Dipper.

ANDROMEDA

Cassiopeia's daughter, Andromeda, was chained to the rocks so that Cetus would be distracted by her, and leave the city alone.

LOOK FOR:
the line of stars which is next to Cassiopeia, and links up to the **Great Square of Pegasus**.

LOOK FOR:
the small arching shape, like a leaping dolphin.

DELPHINUS

A musician charmed this dolphin with a song so that it swam him safely to shore, away from his treacherous shipmates.

ARIES

This magical ram gave away its gleaming golden fleece as a gift, which is why Aries's stars look very faint in the night sky.

LOOK FOR:
a crooked line of faint stars not far from the Pleiades winter cluster in Taurus.

PERSEUS

This hero saw Andromeda chained up after he'd slayed Medusa – a monster whose face turned people to stone. With his eyes shut, he held up Medusa's head, killing the sea monster Cetus stone dead.

LOOK FOR:
the large "Y" shape next to Cassiopeia.

PEGASUS

This winged horse flew out of Medusa's neck when Perseus killed her. An arrogant warrior tried to ride him up to join the gods – but he fell off, so we only see Pegasus among the stars.

To see the positions of these constellations, turn to the star maps on page 30.

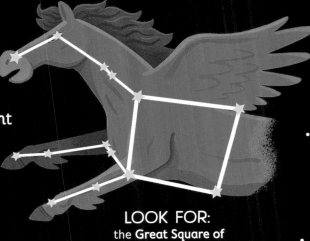

LOOK FOR:
the **Great Square of Pegasus** star pattern.

19

WINTER STARS

Orion, with his sparkling belt, stands out in winter skies. He is surrounded by lots of other brilliant stars, including Sirius — the brightest one of all.

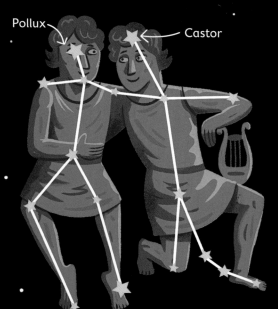

Pollux

Castor

GEMINI

Castor and Pollux were twins with different fathers. Pollux was immortal, but when Castor was killed in battle, Zeus turned them both into stars so that they would be together forever.

LOOK FOR:
the bright stars Castor and Pollux, which make the heads of the twins.

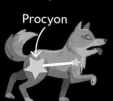

Procyon

CANIS MINOR

This constellation represents the Teumessian Fox — a monstrous beast that could never be caught.

LOOK FOR:
the very bright star Procyon.

CANIS MAJOR

This hunting dog could catch any prey, but one day it was set upon the uncatchable Teumessian Fox. Zeus got so fed up of the endless chase that he hurled them both up into the sky.

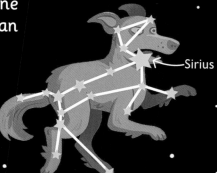

Sirius

LOOK FOR:
the blue-white star Sirius, which is the brightest in the night sky. It's often called the Dog Star.

AURIGA
This legendary chariot racer holds a whip in one hand. The goat that he's carrying fed Zeus, the king of the gods, with her milk when he was a baby.

Capella

LOOK FOR:
its brightest star, Capella, which is also known as the Goat Star.

TAURUS
Zeus sent this bull to carry Princess Europa through the sea to an island. That's why we only see its front half as the waves cover the rest of its body.

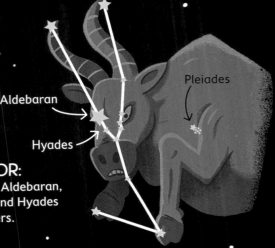

Aldebaran

Pleiades

Hyades

LOOK FOR:
the bright red star Aldebaran, and the Pleiades and Hyades star clusters.

ORION
This giant huntsman boasted that he'd kill every animal alive. In revenge, Gaia the Earth goddess sent a scorpion to kill him, and then put him in the stars to shame him forever.

LOOK FOR:
the line of three stars in **Orion's Belt**, which make Orion very easy to spot.

To see the positions of these constellations, turn to the star maps on page 31.

THE MILKY WAY

Stars exist in gigantic groups called *galaxies*. One of the most spectacular sights you can see is the heart of our own galaxy: the Milky Way.

Scientists think the Milky Way looks like this from the outside, with our Sun on one of its spiral arms.

On a clear, moonless night (summer is best), look south and you'll see a long, misty cloud of millions of stars.

Astronomers thought this starry cloud looked like a trail of milk spilled across the sky, so they called it the Milky Way.

SHOOTING STARS

On a moonless night, you might see a brief streak of light darting across the sky. That's a shooting star. But it's not actually a star at all...

Space dust

Sun

Earth's orbit

Shooting stars are really *meteors* — little bits of space dust that burn up in Earth's atmosphere as they hit it.

When Earth moves through a huge cloud of space dust, you can see showers of hundreds of meteors.

There's a list of the best meteor showers to look for on page 32.

THE MOON

The Moon was probably the first thing that you ever saw in the night sky. But did you know that it's a giant, spinning ball of rock that orbits the Earth?

The Moon spins once each time it orbits our planet, so the same side always faces us – "the near side." The side that we never see from here on Earth is "the far side."

The darker patches on the Moon are called seas. But they're actually huge plains of frozen lava from the Moon's ancient volcanoes.

The bright spots are craters, where space rocks smashed into the Moon billions of years ago.

You can see many of the Moon's seas and craters in detail with just a pair of binoculars.

You've also probably noticed that the Moon appears to change shape. This happens because different amounts of its near side are lit by the Sun as it orbits the Earth.

This diagram shows where light from the Sun hits the surface of the Moon as it orbits the Earth.

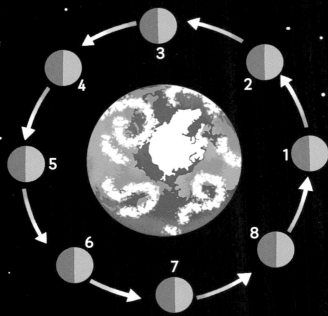

The pictures below show what the Moon looks like from Earth when it's at each of the numbered positions above. These are called the *phases of the Moon*.

1. NEW MOON

2. WAXING CRESCENT

3. FIRST QUARTER

4. WAXING GIBBOUS

5. FULL MOON

6. WANING GIBBOUS

7. THIRD QUARTER

8. WANING CRESCENT

DID YOU KNOW?

The Moon cycles through these phases every 29.5 days, so ancient civilizations used them to make the first calendars. That's where we get the word "month." (Moon-th!)

PLANET HUNTING

The planets reflect sunlight, like the Moon, but they're so far away that they look a lot like stars. Luckily, you can use the rule at the bottom of the page to tell them apart.

Mercury looks like a silvery speck of light in the east just before sunrise, and in the west just after sunset.

Mercury

Venus

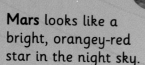

Apart from the Moon, **Venus** shines brightest in the night sky. You can see it for a few hours before dawn and after sunset.

Mars

Mars looks like a bright, orangey-red star in the night sky.

Earth

REMEMBER: if it TWINKLES, it's a STAR...

...but if it SHINES STEADILY, it's a PLANET.

The planets all orbit the Sun at different speeds, so their positions change in relation to the stars. This means they are not always up in the sky when you go looking for them.

Neptune is so far away and so faint that you need a telescope to see it.

Neptune

DID YOU KNOW?
The word "planet" means "wanderer" in Ancient Greek. Early astronomers referred to the planets as 'wandering stars' because they moved much more quickly than the 'fixed' stars.

Uranus

Uranus is on the very limit of what your eyes can see, so you really need binoculars or a telescope to find it.

Huge **Saturn** shines bright and, on really dark nights, you might see a tinge of its golden color.

Saturn

Jupiter is the biggest planet, and it shines pale orange, brighter than any of the stars.

Jupiter

It's easy for computers to predict where the planets will be, so there are lots of websites and apps that show you where to look on any given night.

SPRING STAR MAPS (MARCH TO MAY)

To use these star maps, face either north or south. Then, compare the map for that direction to the stars you can see in the sky.*

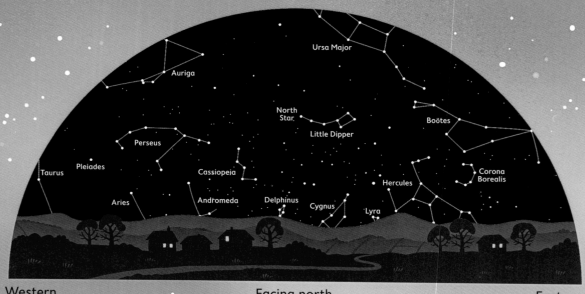

Ursa Major
Auriga
North Star
Little Dipper
Boötes
Perseus
Corona Borealis
Pleiades
Taurus
Cassiopeia
Hercules
Aries
Andromeda
Delphinus
Cygnus
Lyra

Western horizon — Facing north — Eastern horizon

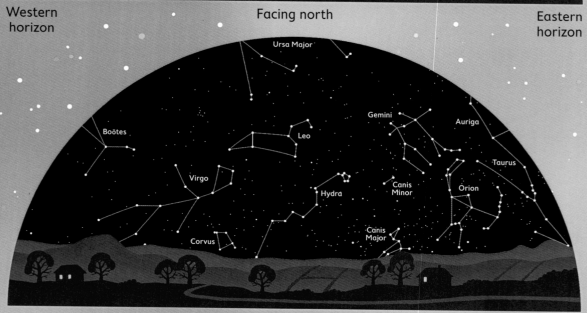

Ursa Major
Gemini
Auriga
Boötes
Leo
Taurus
Virgo
Orion
Hydra
Canis Minor
Corvus
Canis Major

Eastern horizon — Facing south — Western horizon

SUMMER STAR MAPS (JUNE TO AUGUST)

Remember, the stars all appear to turn around the North Star during the night, so you may see these constellations at different angles and positions.

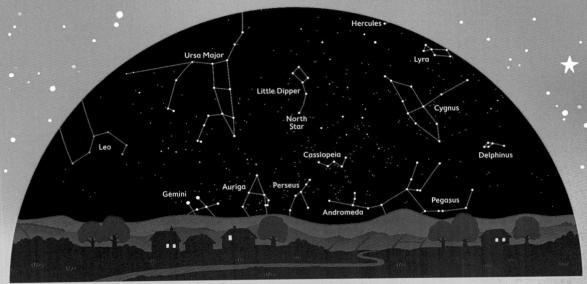

Western horizon   Facing north   Eastern horizon

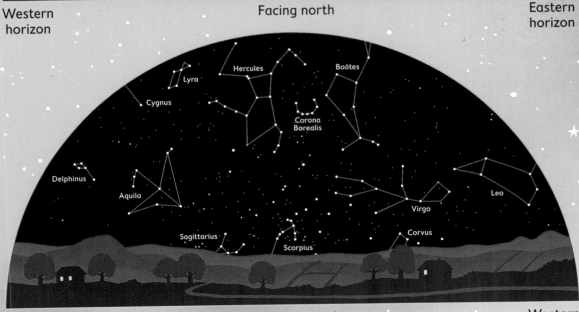

Eastern horizon   Facing south   Western horizon

*These maps are **approximate guides** for where to look from the Northern Hemisphere because your view of the stars changes depending on where you are.

FALL STAR MAPS (SEPTEMBER TO NOVEMBER)

To use these star maps, face either north or south. Then, compare the map for that direction to the stars you can see in the sky.*

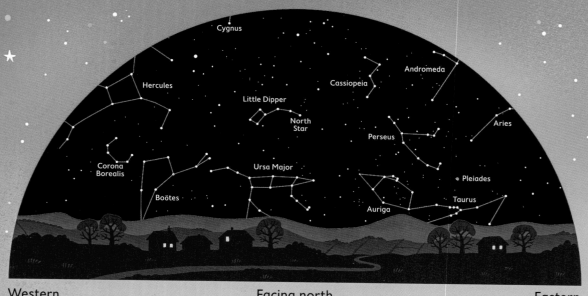

Western horizon

Facing north

Eastern horizon

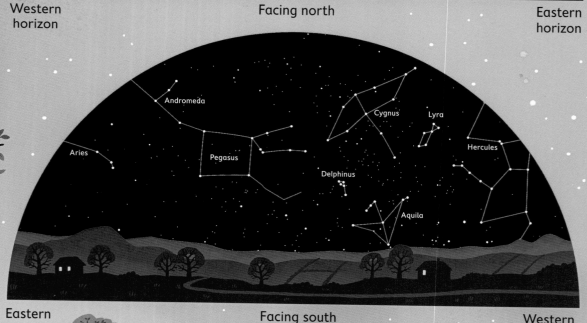

Eastern horizon

Facing south

Western horizon

WINTER STAR MAPS (DECEMBER TO FEBRUARY)

Remember, the stars all appear to turn around the North Star during the night, so you may see these constellations at different angles and positions.

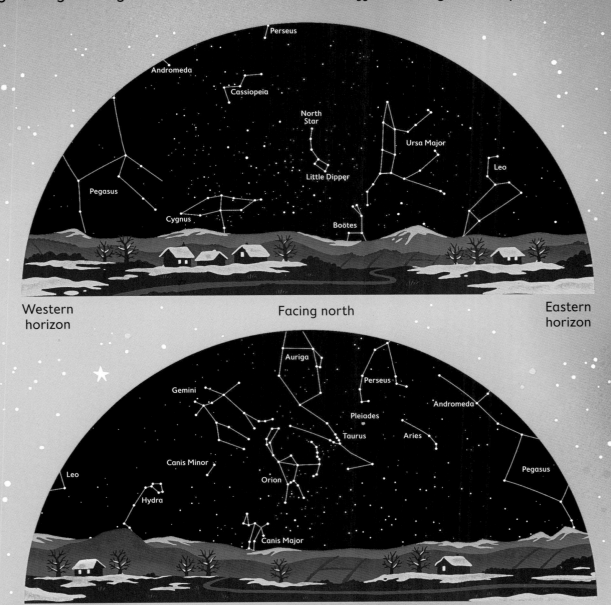

Western horizon

Facing north

Eastern horizon

Eastern horizon

Facing south

Western horizon

*These maps are **approximate guides** for where to look from the Northern Hemisphere because your view of the stars changes depending on where you are.

METEOR SHOWERS TO LOOK OUT FOR

Depending on where you live, you may have to be up very late or early to see some of these.

Name of shower:	Where to look:	When to look:	Peak activity:
Quadrantids	Boötes	December 28th to January 12th	January 4th
Lyrids	Lyra	April 14th to 30th	April 22nd
Perseids	Perseus	July 17th to August 24th	August 12th
Orionids	Orion	October 2nd to November 7th	October 21st
Leonids	Leo	November 6th to 30th	November 18th
Geminids	Gemini	December 4th to 20th	December 14th

INDEX

Edited by Sam Taplin

Picture credits:
p.6 (br) Cynthia Lee / Alamy Stock Photo; p.7 (ml) ESA/Webb, NASA, CSA,
Tom Ray (Dublin); p.9 (br) Razvan Cornel Constantin / Alamy Stock Photo;
p.11 (tr) NASA; p.22 (tr) Science Photo Library / Alamy Stock Photo

With thanks to Stellarium.org for use of their star maps,
and to Steve Hateley for further checking and advice